B532a

AIR MAIL TO THE MOON

AIR MAIL TO THE MOON

by

TOM BIRDSEYE

illustrated by

STEPHEN GAMMELL

Holiday House / New York

TO THE LOOSE-TOOTHED WONDERS
OF SANDPOINT, IDAHO,
THE WRITER'S PROJECT,
AND, ALWAYS, DEBBIE.

My name is Ora Mae Cotton of Crabapple Orchard, and last night somebody stole my tooth.

I'd been down at the creek catching crawdads when it started tingling—kind of like if you missed your toast and peanut butter and bit your teeth really hard instead.

That was three weeks ago.

I was popcorn-in-the-pan excited, for sure that tooth was gonna fall out any second. But Dadaw (that's what I call my daddy) always says not to milk the cow when she's asleep (which is Crabapple Orchard talk for not blabbing to everybody about something before you're sure of what you're blabbing about).

So I didn't tell a soul.

Then last Monday, while fetching the mail at the county road, I stuck my tongue out at my pesky neighbor, Merrietta Bean, and gave her a big raspberry like this— PPLLUBB! The vibration from my tongue flapping against my teeth popped that chomper of mine as loose as a goose on ice skates.

So I told the world about my first tooth coming out . . . whether they wanted to hear or not.

By Thursday that tooth was so wobbly it was just hanging on by one root and a flap of skin. I could push it all the way out between my lips with my tongue *and* help Mama slop the hogs at the same time.

"Oreo," Mama said to me. (Oreo is my nickname, just like the sweet cookie I am.) "Don't flop that tooth out when you're working. It reminds me of your cousin Cyrus before he got braces."

So I kept that tooth inside my mouth, worrying it like mad with my tongue.

Then Friday, right after my big brother Bo Dean and my little sister Kelsey Ann got into a fight at the dinner table over whether Arlene Peterson's pigs really kneel and pray before they eat, that loose tooth of mine fell right out of my mouth—plop—and landed smack in the middle of my spaghetti.

Mama said to be sure and put that tooth under my pillow. That way the tooth fairy would come get it and give me some money. Money! Shoot howdy. Mama didn't say how much. But I figured it had to be at least a thousand dollars, or maybe even a hundred dollars. I was so excited that I hurried to bed as quick as a dropped cat just so I could dream about all the things I was going to buy.

But like I said, somebody stole my tooth. So I guess I dreamed all night for nothing.

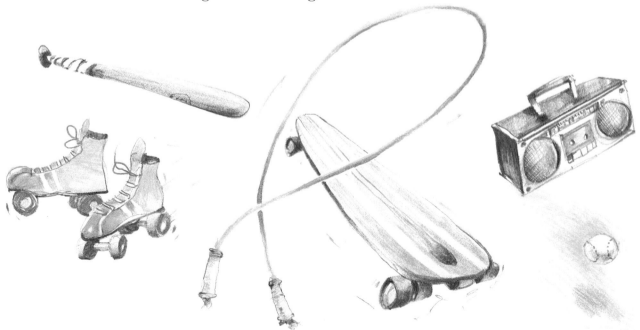

First thing this morning when I discovered the crime, I ran lickety-split to find Mama. She was in the root cellar, up to her elbows in rutabagas.

"Mama!" I exploded, "is the tooth fairy a crook like ol' Hester Jenkins that stole the parking meter from in front of the county courthouse?"

Mama jumped back, eyes as big as sausages. "Why no, Oreo. The tooth fairy is as honest as flowers in the spring."

"That's what I thought," I fumed. "Well, then somebody besides the tooth fairy stole my tooth. Somebody so crooked they screw their socks on every morning. And when I catch 'em, I'm gonna open up a can of gotcha and send 'em airmail to the moon!"

Mama looked at me real hard. "Oreo," she said, "I don't think anybody would steal your tooth. Maybe the tooth fairy is putting it on a string with other teeth to make a beautiful necklace. That's what I've heard she does. She probably forgot to leave you some money and will remember tonight."

That didn't seem likely to me. What good is a tooth fairy that forgets?

"Why don't you go ask your daddy," Mama suggested, seeing how upset I was. "Maybe he knows something we don't."

Aha! I thought. He's a real thinker, my Dadaw is. Why, he even sells watermelons to the grocery store. He knows mighty near everything.

I heard Dadaw before I spied him. He was out by the tire swing shaving and singing at the same time (which is mighty dangerous if you ask me). Half his face was shaving cream. The other half was "as smooth as a baby's belly," as he liked to say.

"Dadaw!" I yelled. "Some crook stole my tooth. And when I catch 'em, I'm gonna open up a can of gotcha and send 'em airmail to the moon!"

Dadaw looked at me real hard. "Oreo," he said, "I don't think anybody would steal your tooth. Maybe the tooth fairy has it and is grinding it up in a big machine. That tooth dust might come out as money. Then the tooth fairy could use it to buy you some real estate. Like one of them condominiums at Miami Beach."

Dadaw sauntered over to the back-porch steps and sat down. He was thinking—about the tooth fairy, money machines, and condominiums, I figured.

It was all a who'd-a-thought-it to me. What would I do with a condominium at Miami Beach?

"Yeah, tooth dust," Dadaw said.

"Tooth dust!?" I kind of shouted. "But Dadaw! Somebody stole my tooth!"

Dadaw rubbed his chin and nodded. "Why don't you go ask your brother. He usually knows more than he tells."

Aha! I thought, heading for the barnyard. My brother
Bo Dean is as ornery as a bull in a beehive. And he lost
two teeth last week when he fell out of the hayloft. I'll bet
he stole my tooth and glued it straight into his mouth.

I'm gonna get that boy, I vowed. And when I do, I'm
gonna open up a can of gotcha and send him airmail to
the moon!

"I didn't steal your tooth, Oreo," brother Bo Dean said calmly, crawling out from under the corn crib. "What would I want with girl teeth, anyway? They don't fit boys."

I hadn't thought of that.

"Are you sure you didn't just give it to the tooth fairy, no money down?"

"Why would I do such a thing!?" I demanded to know. "That's stupid!"

Bo Dean eyed the henhouse. He was looking for his pet snake Fluff. "The tooth fairy saves teeth to give to babies, right, Oreo?"

"Not according to Mama or Dadaw, she don't."

"Well, according to me, Bo Dean Cotton, she does. That's so they can chew on rocks and shoes and stuff."

"Bo Dean, you're ornery!" I reminded him. "Talking about babies like that."

"Yep," he whispered as he snuck in the henhouse door. "But I'm right. Where do you think sister Kelsey Ann got her teeth when she was little?"

Aha! I thought. Maybe Bo Dean has a point. Kelsey Ann is as ornery as Bo Dean plus ten. She *had* to be the one that stole my tooth.

"I'll get that little diddle-do!" I roared.

"The tooth fairy?" Bo Dean asked, sticking his head out of the chicken house, Fluff in one hand, scared-hairy chickens squawking and flying everywhere.

"No! Kelsey Ann Cotton," I snapped. "And when I do, I'm gonna open up a can of gotcha and send her air-mail to the moon!"

"Kelsey Ann Cotton!" I yelled up the backyard apple tree. "Give me my tooth. I know you stole it."

"Pig feathers," she said, hanging upside down from her knees on a tree limb. "I'm as sweet as roses in the snow. The tooth fairy steals teeth, not me. She makes them into doorknobs. Didn't you know that, Oreo?"

"Not according to Mama, Dadaw, or Bo Dean she doesn't. You took it!" I shrieked.

"She does too, 'cause I didn't," Kelsey Ann snipped.

"Does not, you did!"

"Does too, I didn't."

"Does not, you did!"

Kelsey Ann giggled. "I'll bet you threw it away, Oreo. It's probably in the bottom of the garbage can stuck in the middle of a blob of leftover spaghetti. That's how forgetful you are. That tooth will never be a doorknob."

That did it. I was so mad I was ready to scream. *Nobody* really knew what the tooth fairy was up to. *Nobody* was a bit of help. And *nobody* was the lop-eared rascal that stole my tooth. I was just about to pop my cork clean out of Crabapple Orchard. That's how mad I was.

But instead, I just stood there looking at my upside-down sister, and I started crying—loud and long, big tears streaming down my face tasting like salt.

I didn't want to cry. I just couldn't stop.

Now, we Cottons banter, shout, squabble, and argue at one another a fair amount—just like any self-respecting family. But if it ever comes to a Cotton bawling real tears of grief, the rest come a-running to help hey-ho-howdy in a flash. Dadaw, Mama, Bo Dean, Kelsey Ann, and even my pesky little neighbor Merrietta Bean were all at my side in five seconds flat.

"Somebody stole my tooth," I sobbed, crying harder than ever, "and when I catch'em I'm gonna open up a can of gotcha and send 'em airmail to the moon."

And I stuck my hands down deep in my pockets, trying to look like I meant it.

My name is Ora Mae Cotton of Crabapple Orchard. My face is hot. My toes are curling. And right now I feel like a possum up a plum tree. I'm as embarrassed as a zebra without stripes.

You see, there's this little hard thing in the bottom of my pants pocket. It's right where I left it.

I wonder if the tooth fairy ever sends motor-mouth kids like me airmail to the moon.

Text copyright © 1988 by Tom Birdseye
Illustrations copyright © 1988 by Stephen Gammell
Printed in the United States of America
First Edition

Library of Congress Cataloging-in-Publication Data

Birdseye, Tom.
Airmail to the Moon.

SUMMARY: When the tooth that she was saving for the
tooth fairy disappears, Ora Mae sets out to find the
thief and send him "airmail to the moon!"
  [1. Teeth—Fiction.   2. Tooth fairy—Fiction]
I. Gammell, Stephen, ill.   II. Title.
PZ7.B5213Ai   1988   [E]   87-21199
ISBN 0-8234-0683-0